FOR NIKTA AND MOHSEN

SIMON & SCHUSTER BOOKS FOR YOUNG READERS

An imprint of Simon & Schuster Children's Publishing Division

1230 Avenue of the Americas, New York, New York 10020

© 2022 by Sina Merabian

Book design by Lucy Ruth Cummins © 2022 by Simon & Schuster, Inc.

For information about special discounts for bulk purchases, please contact Simon & Schuster
Special Sales at 1-866-506-1949 or business@simonandschuster.com.

The Simon & Schuster Speakers Bureau can bring authors to your live event. For more
information or to book an event, contact the Simon & Schuster Speakers Bureau at
1-866-248-3049 or visit our website at www.simonspeakers.com.

The text for this book was set in Aunt Mildred.

The illustrations for this book were rendered in Photoshop and Procreate.

Manufactured in China

1121 SCP

First Edition

2 4 6 8 10 9 7 5 3 1

Library of Congress Cataloging-in-Publication Data

Names: Merabian, Sina, author, illustrator. | Merabian, Sina, illustrator.

Title: The monster in the bathhouse / Sina Merabian.

Description: First edition. | New York : Simon & Schuster Books for Young Readers, 2022.

Audience: Ages 4-8. | Audience: Grades K-1. | Summary: In an Iranian
bathhouse on the eve of Nowruz, three boys suspect a Div—a monster—is wreaking havoc
on their New Year preparations.

Identifiers: LCCN 2020050035 (print) | LCCN 2020050036 (ebook)

ISBN 9781534496828 (hardcover) | ISBN 9781534496835 (ebook)

Subjects: CYAC: Nawrūz (Festival)—Fiction. | New Year—Fiction. | Monsters—Fiction. |
Bathhouses—Fiction.

Classification: LCC PZ7.1.M4735 Mo 2022 (print) | LCC PZ7.1.M4735 (ebook) |
DDC [E]—dc23

LC record available at https://lccn.loc.gov/2020050035

LC ebook record available at https://lccn.loc.gov/2020050036

THE MONSTER IN THE BATHHOUSE

WRITTEN & ILLUSTRATED BY SINA MERABIAN

SIMON & SCHUSTER BOOKS FOR YOUNG READERS

New York London Toronto Sydney New Delhi

The bathhouse is always busy the day before Nowruz. Everyone wants to be clean for the new year.

To celebrate, the bathhouse passes out tea and sweets.

They've even set up their own Haft-sin . . .

with special items to say hello to spring.

"What was that?"

"Maybe we should stay here."

Something **very big**
has taken a bath . . .

with very large
feet to break all
the pumices . . .

and very sharp
horns to rip all
the loofahs. . . .

It's a Div! With big horns! And big, dirty feet!

It's come to ruin Nowruz!

The fathers have
a good laugh.
"A monster?"
"In our bathhouse?"
"We'll teach it a
lesson!"

But . . .

It's a . . .

Meoooww!

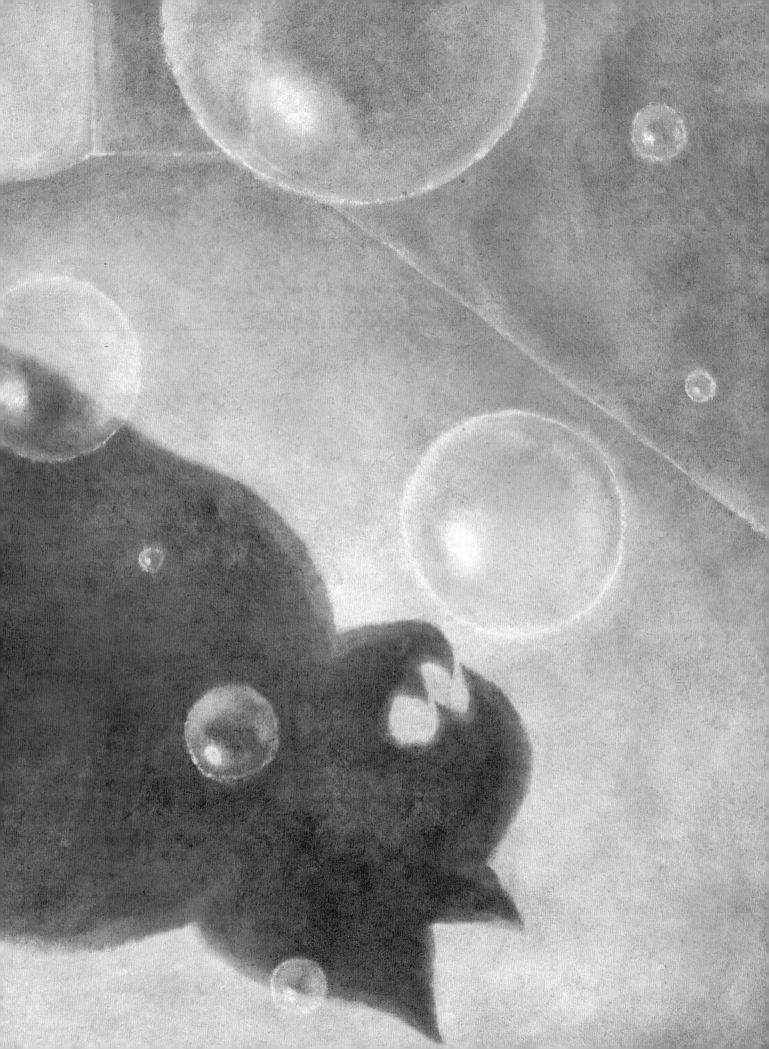

For the rest of the day, everyone knows
what story they'll be sharing on Nowruz.

"What an adventure!"

On Nowruz, *everyone* celebrates the new year.